The Art Lesson

A Shavuot Story

To Burt & Rita Marks, Chet Geary, and in loving memory of Judith Geary —A. and W. Marks

To Matt and our two true works of art, Abraham and Grace —A.W.

KAR-BEN PUBLISHING
A division of Lerner Publishing Group, Inc.
241 First Avenue North
Minneapolis, MN 55401 USA
1-800-4-KARBEN

Website address: www.karben.com

Main body text set in Billy Infant Regular 15/20.

Library of Congress Cataloging-in-Publication Data

Names: Marks, Allison, author. | Marks, Wayne, author. | Wilkinson, Annie, illustrator.
Title: The art lesson : a Shavuot story / by Allison & Wayne Marks ; illustrated by Annie Wilkinson.
Description: Minneapolis, Minneapolis : Kar-Ben Publishing, [2016] | 2016 | Age 3-8, K to grade 3.
Identifiers: LCCN 2016008979 (print) | LCCN 2016009596 (ebook) | ISBN 9781467781725 (lb : alk. paper) | ISBN 9781467781732 (pb : alk. paper) | ISBN 9781512427202 (eb pdf)
Subjects: | CYAC: Shavuot—Juvenile fiction.
Classification: LCC PZ7.M34175 Art 2016 (print) | LCC PZ7.M34175 (ebook) | DDC [E]—dc23

Back matter photographs are used with the permission of: Library of Congress LC-USZ62-116611 (Marc Chagall); REX Shutterstock (Amedeo Modigliani); © Ernst Haas/Getty Images (Lee Krasner); Wikimedia Commons (Camille Pissarro).

LC record available at http://lccn.loc.gov/2016008979

Manufactured in China
1-37785-19030-11/2/2016

051716.4K1/B1046/A7

The Art Lesson

A Shavuot Story

By Allison & Wayne Marks
Illustrated by Annie Wilkinson

Every Thursday after school, Shoshana rushed home and slipped on her art smock. Drips of dried blue and silver paint ran down its sleeves. Splotches of pink and purple exploded like fireworks across the front. Bits of clay, gold glitter, sequins, flecks of crushed crayons, and streaks of ink covered it from top to bottom.

Shoshana loved her smock. Each splatter, smudge, and stain reminded her of art projects she made in Grandma Jacobs' art studio: a miniature sukkah made of toothpicks, a lopsided dreidel that always landed on *gimel*, a Purim grogger. She wondered excitedly what new memory she would add today.

As Shoshana put on her black beret, she heard three beeps from a car horn. “Grandma J’s here!” Shoshana cried. She grabbed her box of art supplies and ran outside.

Grandma Jacobs opened the passenger door. "Is my little Chagall ready to be creative today?"

"You bet!" Shoshana said.

"Outstanding! Let's go make something beautiful!"

For Shoshana, Grandma J's art studio was like an enchanted forest. Bold masks dotted the walls. Mobiles of birds and bats, balloons and butterflies dangled from the ceiling. Painted vines covered the wooden floor.

Paintbrushes sprouted like weeds from glass jars. Every corner was filled with easels, canvases, tubes of oil paint, and pads of paper as big as Shoshana.

Near the patio door stood a large cabinet with a hundred small drawers—ten rows up and ten rows across. Before each art lesson, Grandma J let Shoshana open one drawer to see what treasure lay inside.

Shoshana had already opened nearly every drawer, discovering coins, buttons, vials of sand, skeleton keys, plastic dinosaurs, hair ribbons, postage stamps, pine cones, seashells, and beads of all sorts.

“See that drawer at the very top right?” Grandma Jacobs asked. “Go ahead and see what’s inside. You’ll need to use the stepstool.”

Inside the drawer were square sheets of paper. Shoshana held one up and examined it. "What's so special about this?" she asked.

"Come, my little artist," Grandma J said. "Sit with me on the sofa and let me show you."

Grandma J folded one of the sheets into a small square. “This is something my bubbe taught me how to do when I was a little girl.”

With a pencil, Grandma J drew shapes along each edge of the folded paper.

Next, she cut out each shape with a pair of scissors. Flakes of paper fluttered to the floor, frosting Shoshana's shoes like snow.

Grandma J made a final cut and opened the folded paper. Shoshana let out a gasp of delight. "It's beautiful!" she exclaimed. The plain paper had changed into a Star of David surrounded by birds.

“Thank you, my little Modigliani,” Grandma Jacobs said. “When I was growing up, families on our street would hang papercuts like these in our windows to decorate for Shavuot.”

Grandma J carefully lifted three papercuts from a wooden chest. Shoshana's eyes widened.

"On Shavuot we celebrate the spring harvest."

"This one shows God's gift of the Torah. Some people stay up all night studying Torah on the night before Shavuot."

"This papercut is for you, Shoshana. Your name means 'rose' in Hebrew."

"I love it!" Shoshana said. "I want to make a bouquet of roses, too!"

And for the rest of the afternoon, that's what Shoshana tried to do.

Snippets of paper flew everywhere—landing in her hair, filling the pocket of her smock, and covering Krasner, her grandmother's calico cat.

But no matter how many times Shoshana folded and snipped, traced and trimmed, she didn't see roses when she opened up her creations. All she saw were papers filled with holes.

Grandma J saw Shoshana set down her scissors and cross her arms in frustration. "May I see what you've done?"

She gathered Shoshana's cut-outs and taped them to the patio door. The late afternoon sun shined through. "Oh, my little Pissarro," Grandma J said, "These are fabulous!"

Grandma J pointed to a papercut. "What do you see when you look at this one?" she asked. Shoshana frowned and shrugged.

"It reminds me of the time we saw a flock of geese flying over the lake," her grandmother said.

Shoshana looked closer. A hint of a smile appeared on her face. This time, she pointed to one of the papercuts. "Here's a honeycomb filled with bees!"

“Yes! I see it, too!” Grandma J exclaimed, giving Shoshana a high-five. Suddenly, Shoshana could see pirate ships, fields of flowers, schools of fish, and hot air balloons.

Grandma J bent down and gently cupped Shoshana's chin. "See? Every papercut is different. Every papercut is special. Just like you."

At home, Shoshana taped her papercuts to her bedroom windows to decorate for Shavuot. She hung up her smock and smiled.

Many, many Shavuot holidays passed, and Shoshana became a grandmother herself. Every Thursday after school, her granddaughter, Hannah, came to her studio wearing a smock and a beret, ready for an art lesson. "Grandma S, which drawer should I open this time?" Hannah asked as she stood before the large cabinet.

"Try the one at the very top right," Shoshana replied.

Hannah climbed the stepstool and opened the drawer, pulling out square sheets of paper.

"I've been saving those for a special art lesson," Shoshana said. "Come, my little Chagall. Sit with me on the sofa and let me show you."

A Note About Shavuot and Papercuts

On Shavuot the Jewish people celebrate receiving the Ten Commandments, and thank God for the first fruits of the spring harvest, such as figs, wheat, dates, olives, grapes, and pomegranates. It is also traditional to eat foods made with milk and honey, such as blintzes, cheesecake, and honey cake. The Jews of Eastern Europe made papercuts to hang in their windows for Shavuot. These folk art pieces often included Hebrew words and rosettes, called *roizalakh* in Yiddish. Other popular images include Torah scrolls, the Tree of Life, lions, tigers, birds, and other animals.

Star of David Papercut

1) Take an 8 inch/20 cm square piece of paper and fold it in half to make a rectangle.
2) Fold the rectangle into a square.
3) Using safety scissors, cut out the shapes as shown. The star must be cut on the main fold.
4) Unfold and hang in your window.

* You can also cut the folded paper any way you'd like. Use your imagination to see what you have made!

"My Little Chagall"

Grandma Jacobs called Shoshana by several nicknames. Each one—Chagall, Modigliani, Pissarro—is the name of a famous Jewish artist. Grandma Jacobs even named her cat Krasner, after a Jewish painter. Art has always been an important part of Jewish culture expressing life's joys and sorrows.

Marc Chagall

Marc Chagall (1887-1985) painted vivid, dream-like scenes of goats and fiddlers, towering blue roosters and rabbis, circuses and flying ghostly figures. He filled many of his paintings and stained glass windows with his memories of growing up in Vitebsk, Russia. ***You can see art in the style of Chagall as the background on page 7.***

Amedeo Modigliani

Amedeo Modigliani (1884-1920) was born in Italy and later moved to France, where he became known for painting and sculpting portraits of men and women featuring mask-like faces and long necks. ***You can see art in the style of Modigliani in the portrait on page 17 and on the wall on page 28.***

Lee Krasner

Lee Krasner (1908-1984), an American artist, painted bright swirls and shapes, rows of black and white squares, and patterns from nature. Krasner expressed her emotions through her paintings, allowing viewers to feel what they saw on the canvas in their own way. ***You can see art in the style of Krasner on the wall on page 20.***

Camille Pissarro

Camille Pissarro (1830-1903) painted realistic scenes of life in France such as a busy marketplace, a street lit up at night, and workers harvesting hay. Known as an "Impressionist" painter, he used small brushstrokes and sometimes dots to capture brief moments in time. ***You can see art in the style of Pissarro in the natural view through the window (not a painting) on page 22.***